THE EVENT

DANIEL GRANT

PART 8

NO ONE UNDER THE AGE OF CONSENT, IN WHATEVER JURISDICTION YOU HAPPEN TO FIND YOURSELF, SHOULD EVEN CONSIDER READING THIS COMIC. IF YOU DO, IT'S VERY LIKELY TO PERMANANTLY SHRIVEL YOUR SEX ORGANS.

YOU'VE BEEN WARNED.

THIS COMIC CONTAINS ALL THE GOOD STUFF, NUDITY, SEX AND VIOLENCE. IF ANY OF THE ABOVE CAUSE YOU ANGST --

PLEASE DO NOT READ ANY FURTHER.

ISBN-13: 978-1-948297-23-3

DALLENT

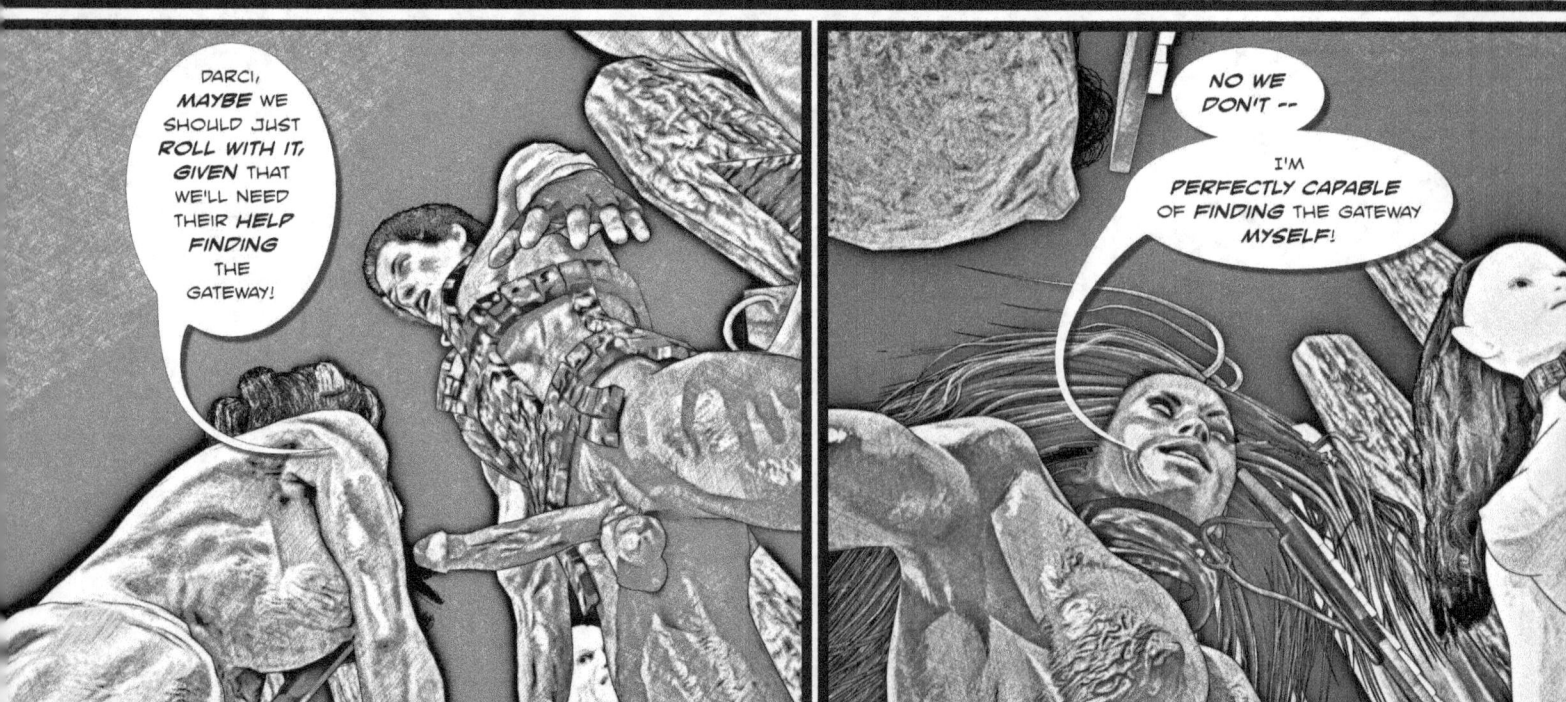

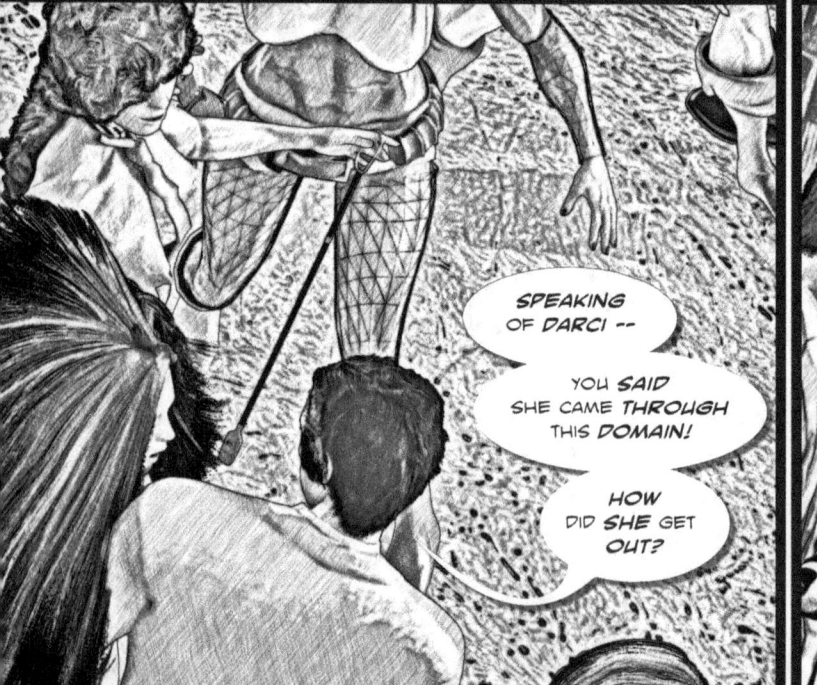

www.ingramcontent.com/pod-product-compliance
Lightning Source LLC
Chambersburg PA
CBHW082017170626

46817CB00009B/3130